Pet Detectives
The Ball Burglary

Written by Jana Hunter

Illustrated by Kim Blundell

Collins

Lost a pet? Seen a pet crime?
Then you need the Pet Detectives!
Pet Detectives find pets ...
they stop crimes.
But sometimes *pets* can solve crimes too!
How do I know?
I am a Pet Detective and ...
this is the story of what my pet did.

2

It all started when I got a text from my pal Chas.
I was just reading it when …
scratch!
Then more scratches.
Scratch! Scratch! Scratch!

My dog, Rooney, was scratching at the door.
(I know – I'm a detective.)
I pulled open the door. "Rooney!"
Rooney pounced on me. "Ooof!"
He landed. I fell.

4

"Rooney, get off!" I laughed.
But Rooney wouldn't leave me alone.
He was trying to tell me something.
(I know because I'm a detective.)

Then Rooney bounded over to the window,
and I saw that it was wide open.

"Uh-oh ... " I got up. "This might be a crime, Rooney,"
I said in my best detective voice. "Someone has been
in here and opened this window. Who did it?"
But Rooney just wanted to go outside and play.

Now Rooney is a very clever dog.

He leapt down from the window and begged.

I knew that look.

He wanted to play ball.

I wanted to know who had opened the window.

7

But Rooney wouldn't listen.
"OK," I said, "you win. Let's go and play ball."
(Rooney is like me and Chas – football mad.)
So I looked for my football …
and so did Rooney.

I looked on top of the cupboard.
I looked under my bed.

I looked *in* the cupboard.

I looked *in* my bed!
But it was no good.
My best United ball was gone! Gone, gone gone …
and the window was open!
"This is a case for a detective," I told Rooney.

"Who took my ball?"

At the word "ball", Rooney grabbed the end of my United scarf.

"Yes, I know you want to go out and play," I said.

"But first we must solve the Ball Burglary." (Rooney may be the cleverest dog in the world, but even he can get things wrong.)

I wrote in my notebook:

1. An open window
2. A missing football

Rooney leapt up to the window again.
And that was when I saw it.
The footprint.
The dirty, big footprint, right there on the windowsill …
"Aha!" I said. "A clue."

Who did that?

"I bet the ball burglar did it," I thought.
"Find the ball burglar and his footprint
will match this footprint."
"Rooney, did you see who took my ball?" I asked.
Rooney was wagging his tail.
"OK, Rooney," I said. "We *will* play. But we have to
find the ball first."

12

But Rooney wouldn't budge.
Was he trying to tell me something?
He was!
Because there was my next clue.
(Detectives are good at finding clues.)
The clue was a bubblegum wrapper.
A purple *Bubble-Bubble* bubblegum wrapper,
just below the window.

"Hmmm, *Bubble-Bubble*," I said. I leant out and
picked it up.

"Chas's favourite bubblegum."

I flipped open my notebook. I wrote down all the clues
to the Ball Burglary:

1. An open window

2. A missing football

3. A footprint

4. A Bubble-Bubble bubblegum wrapper

Then I smelt a familiar smell.

"Rooney, can you smell what I smell?" I said.

"*Blackberry Bubble-Bubble* bubblegum. Chas's favourite
flavour!"

And just as I was writing down this clue,
the next clue came.
A rustle in the bushes!

I ran to the window again. There, in the garden next
door, was Chas's pet python, Jaws. Chas's greedy snake.
He hadn't been eating *Bubble-Bubble* bubblegum, but he'd
eaten something else …

He'd eaten something round.
(I could tell from the bulge in his middle –
the ball-shaped bulge!)
"My ball!"

So Jaws was the thief. A snake! He had swallowed
my ball.
My best United football.
But Rooney was still trying to tell me something.
He was pawing at the footprint on the window ledge
and barking.
"What is it, Rooney?"

I looked closely at the footprint clue again.

Suddenly I got it!

I got what Rooney was trying to tell me.

Snakes don't leave footprints!

(I'm a pet detective, I know about pets.)

I smelled that bubblegum smell again ...

"I know," I laughed. "It's ...

"CHAS!"

My pal Chas jumped up out of the bushes – and guess what he was holding?

My best United football.

"Bingo!"

CHAS!

Woof!

"It was you!" I laughed. "You took my ball!"
"I *had* to," said Chas. "Jaws swallowed *my* ball!
I borrowed yours so we could play!"
"Rooney tried to tell me it was you all along," I said.
"Rooney, the Pet Detective!" Chas laughed.
"Clever boy." I hugged my dog. "You helped solve
the crime."

19

Chas picked Jaws up and stroked his fat tummy. "Never mind, Jaws, the air will come out of the ball soon and you'll feel better. Want to play football?" he asked me.

Rooney went wild when he heard the word "ball" again.

So we ran downstairs and out into the garden.

Two Pet Detectives and one pal – the best team ever.

But Jaws didn't want to play football.

He'd had enough for one day!

The Ball Burglary

23

Ideas for guided reading

Learning objectives: Identifying and describing characters, expressing own views and using words and phrases from texts; identifying speech marks in reading, understand their purpose, use the terms correctly; using phonological, contextual, grammatical and graphic knowledge to work out, predict and check the meanings of unfamiliar words and to make sense of what they read.

Curriculum links: Animals and us

Interest words: detective, solve, burglary, crime, Rooney, pounced, clue, footprint, familiar, favourite, python, thief, swallowed, borrowed

Word count: 878

Getting started

- Read the title to the group, checking that all the children know what 'burglary' means. Looking at the cover picture, ask the children to make predictions and talk about the characters. *What can you say about the Pet Detective and his dog?* Use some of the interest words in the discussion, e.g. *I think the Pet Detective has a new **crime** to **solve**.*

- Ask the children to read the blurb aloud, working as a group to solve 'tricky' words on the run. *How might the Pet Detective's dog help him?*

Reading and responding

- Read p2 together, emphasizing the effects of question and exclamation marks. Ask the children to say what they noticed about these effects.

- Invite the children to say what they know about the character and say how they know (they may remember him from *Tortoise Trouble* or make inferences from the pictures). Talk about the kind of 'voice' he might have. Ask a volunteer to demonstrate how the Pet Detective might say the words on p3. Praise any expression used.

- As they read on to see if the Pet Detective can solve the crime, listen to individuals read aloud in turn. Prompt them to comment on the characters and alter their voices to show differences. Talk about the effects of speech marks and speech bubbles.